Best
Christmas
Ever

hardie grant EGMONT

Best Christmas Ever
first published in 2005
this edition published in 2011 by
Hardie Grant Egmont
Ground Floor, Building 1, 658 Church Street
Richmond, Victoria 3121, Australia
www.hardiegrantegmont.com.au

A CiP record for this title is available from the National Library of Australia

Illustration by Aki Fukuoka
Design by Michelle Mackintosh
Text design and typesetting by Ektavo

Printed in Australia by Griffin Press, an Accredited ISO AS/NZS
14001:2004 Environmental Management System printer.

3 5 7 9 10 8 6 4 2

The paper this book is printed on is certified against
Forest Stewardship Council® Standards. Griffin Press holds
FSC chain of custody certification SGS-COC-005088. FSC
promotes environmentally responsible, socially beneficial
and economically viable management of the world's forests.

FSC
www.fsc.org
MIX
Paper from
responsible sources
FSC® C009448

go girl

WITHDRAWN

Best

Christmas Ever

by
Rowan McAuley

Illustrations by
Aki Fukuoka

hardie grant EGMONT

Chapter One

Ching Ching loved Christmas. It was her favourite time of the year, when everything seemed just a little bit magical.

She loved it at night when the house was dark and the fairy lights on the Christmas tree made the living room flash with different colours. She loved the gingerbread house, all decorated with tiny silver balls and white icing, that stood on the hall table until her mum finally gave in and said they could eat it.

She loved all the delicious and special food they had at Christmas — prawns, mango ice-cream, fruit salad with pineapple, peppermint candy canes, pieces of chocolate wrapped in gold foil to look like pirate treasure ...

But most of all, she loved the family Christmas shopping trip into the city, the day before Christmas Eve. Dad called it 'Eve Eve'. And the best thing about the shopping trip was that it was tonight!

Ching Ching had been buzzing with excitement ever since she got up. She giggled and sang all through breakfast.

'Watch out!' said her dad, as she knocked the milk over with her elbow.

She skipped and danced all through lunch.

'Ow! Careful!' said her mum, as Ching Ching leapt past the table and landed on her foot.

She chattered like a monkey and jumped up and down on the spot until her brothers William, Henry and Daniel all yelled at her and told her to be quiet. And that was pretty amazing because William, Henry and Daniel were very noisy themselves.

But Ching Ching couldn't help it. She couldn't sit still and she couldn't be calm. It was the most exciting night of the year (well, second to Christmas Eve) she had butterflies in her tummy.

Except they were too big to be

butterflies. Ching Ching thought they were more like seagulls. Yes! Like seagulls at the park when you throw them a chip and they all go crazy, flapping their wings and fighting for it.

She went to her room and tried to read a book, but she couldn't concentrate. Not even *The Black Stallion* could hold her attention. She wanted to talk to someone about how much fun the shopping trip was going to be, but her mum was busy weeding, her dad was in the study working, and her brothers had already told her to leave them alone.

Ching Ching phoned her best friend Olivia, but no-one answered. She tried to phone her friend Iris, but her mum said Iris was out with her dad. Ching Ching didn't know anyone else's number off by heart.

She decided to go for a swim. She practised her underwater handstands and somersaults. She was seeing how long she could sit on the bottom of the pool, holding her breath, when she heard her dad yelling over the pool fence.

'Out you get, kiddo!' he called, as she shook water out of her ears. 'It's time to get ready. The boys are all dressed and want to get going.'

Chapter Two

Ching Ching raced inside and quickly put on her best clothes, while her mum jiggled the car keys and her brothers chanted, 'Come on, Ching Ching! Hurry up!'

At last everyone was ready. They all piled into the car and drove to the train station. Once they had their tickets, they galloped downstairs to the station platform just as a train to the city arrived.

Their adventure had properly started! As the train doors closed, Ching Ching breathed a sigh of relief.

The boys found two empty bench seats. Ching Ching squeezed in between Henry and the window.

'Ooh! There doesn't seem to be as much room on these seats as last year,' said her dad, sitting down.

'Well, don't look at us,' said William. 'It's Ching Ching who's grown so much.'

'Yes,' said Henry, pinching her arm playfully. 'Look at how big and muscly she is.'

'Stop it,' said Ching Ching, trying to sound cross but giggling as William tickled her. 'It's you boys who are taking up all the space!'

That was true. William, Henry and Daniel were all tall, with big, square shoulders and huge arms. Ching Ching looked like a little string of spaghetti squashed in there.

'Ah, you're growing up so quickly,' said her mum fondly, a little tear in her eye. 'You're all changing so much.'

Ching Ching frowned. She wished her mum wouldn't say things like that. She didn't want things to change. She wanted them to always be together, just as they were right now.

'Don't cry, Mum,' said William. 'I'm going to live at home until I'm thirty, and you can still do my washing.'

'Yeah,' said Daniel, 'and I want you to tuck me into bed and read me stories even when I'm forty.'

'And you can still do that thing where you spit on a tissue and wipe my face until

I'm at least fifty,' added Henry.

Mum made a face at Ching Ching's brothers. 'All right, very funny,' she said. 'Go and grow up! Don't worry about me.'

Dad patted her knee. 'Don't tease your poor old mum too much, boys,' he said. 'She still has to buy us all dinner.'

'Hey, look!' said Ching Ching. 'It's our station. It's time to get off!'

When the doors opened Ching Ching stepped out onto the platform and breathed in the stuffy, smelly air of the station.

They were in the city!

Chapter Three

Ching Ching's eyes were shining with excitement. Normally she didn't like the city much. It was too dull and grey, with ugly concrete buildings and cross-looking people in a hurry. But at Christmas, even the city seemed special.

Everything was just as Ching Ching remembered from last year, except maybe better. The shop windows were decorated

with lights and Christmas trees, and the trees in the street were lit up with tiny silver lights. Even the people walking past seemed happier and less rushed than usual.

Ahead on the street corner, a woman dressed all in white and wearing angel wings was handing out flowers and smiling at everyone.

In the other direction, there were grown-up people wearing business suits and reindeer antlers on their heads!

'Come on,' said Ching Ching's dad. 'Let's get the shopping over and done with – I can't wait for dinner!'

They started walking towards the big department stores, winding their way through the crowds. It was difficult for six people to walk together so they were in twos. William and Daniel were up ahead – Ching Ching could see their blond heads sticking up above the rest of the crowd. Then came her mum and Henry, trying to catch William and Daniel. Last of all came Ching Ching and her dad, holding hands.

Even though her dad had said he wanted to get the shopping over and done with, he didn't seem to be in a hurry. They wandered happily, looking in the different shops and pointing things out to each other.

'Look over there, Ching Ching. Have you ever seen a girl with such long curly hair?' asked her dad.

'Look at that dog with a Santa hat on!' laughed Ching Ching.

Ching Ching realised the city really was an interesting place. Some people were smartly dressed, like they were on their way to a party. Others were just in ordinary clothes, like they came to the city all the time.

Suddenly, out of the corner of her eye, Ching Ching saw a curious thing. In the narrow space between two shops a man sat on a milk crate. He had a blanket over his knees. On the ground beside him was a cardboard box with the words 'Make a Christmas wish' written on the side. Inside the box were some coins and a $5 note.

The man was just sitting there, watching the people go by. When he saw Ching Ching looking at him he winked at her and waved in a friendly way. Ching Ching clutched hold of her dad's hand.

Before she could say something to her dad, they had already walked past, and the man on the milk crate was left behind.

'Almost there,' said her dad. 'Just one more block to the store.'

Ching Ching looked around. The streets were still bright and cheerful, but somehow everything looked less magical, somehow less perfect, than it did a moment ago.

Everyone was walking along, thinking about Christmas and shopping and having a good time, but Ching Ching couldn't stop thinking about that man, alone on the footpath with his box of Christmas wishes.

Chapter Four

'Dad,' said Ching Ching, as they waited for the lights to change. 'Did you see that man back there?'

'No. What man?' asked her dad.

'There was a man back there, sitting on a milk crate,' said Ching Ching.

'Was he sick? Did he need help?' Her dad turned, as if to go back and see.

'I don't know,' said Ching Ching. 'He

didn't exactly look sick. He just looked a bit sad. He was sitting under a blanket.'

'Oh,' said her dad. 'He was probably homeless.'

'Homeless?' said Ching Ching.

'Yes, there are some people who live on the streets because they have nowhere else to go.'

Ching Ching thought about this.

'Why doesn't he just go and stay with his mum and dad?' she asked.

'Well, not everyone *has* a mum and dad.'

'What about his brothers and sisters, then?' asked Ching Ching.

Her dad didn't say anything.

'You mean, he might be on his own at

Christmas?' she asked, biting her lip.

'He might be,' said her dad.

'That's terrible!' said Ching Ching.

'I know, darling,' said her dad in a gentle voice. 'Look, the lights have changed. Let's go meet the others.'

How awful to be lonely at Christmas!

On the other side of the street her mum and brothers were waiting outside the department store. The windows were a blaze of light and colour, just like last year. People were queuing to see the displays.

'Come and see!' said her mum. 'They've got a terrific set-up of Santa's workshop, with moving elves!'

She took Ching Ching's hand and together they went up close to the glass. Her mum was right – the windows looked great.

There was a tiny train pulling carriages of brightly wrapped presents. There were little elves in green and red, set up to look like they were hammering and painting the toys in front of them. And at the back, watching the whole thing, was a fat, jolly Santa, smiling and laughing.

'Isn't it fabulous?' asked her mum. 'Even better than last year.'

Ching Ching smiled. She could see that it was all very pretty. It was exactly the sort of thing that she would have loved any other day.

But she couldn't stop thinking about the homeless man. When she saw all the happy faces, she thought about how sad she would be if she were alone on Christmas Day.

Chapter Five

After they had looked at the windows, they all went inside. They split up as usual – Ching Ching went with her mum and her brothers went with her dad.

'Meet you back here in an hour,' said her dad, as Henry and Daniel dragged him away.

'Let's look at the dolls first,' her mum suggested.

Ching Ching nodded.

Upstairs in the toy department, the special Christmas dolls were on display. Delicate china dolls, with long hair and silk dresses, sat in rows on the shelves.

Each one had a beautifully painted face. A blonde Russian doll with a black fur hat sat next to a red-headed doll in a tartan dress, and next to her was a fairy doll with wings and a wand.

'Look at this one,' said her mum. 'She reminds me of you!'

Ching Ching's mum was holding up a cheeky-looking doll with long black hair.

'Oh, yes,' said Ching Ching. 'Very nice.'

'All right,' said her mum. 'What's going

on? You've hardly said a word since we got here, and the dolls are usually your favourite thing of all!'

'Well,' said Ching Ching. 'I saw a homeless man on the way here, and Dad said that some people have no family, and that even on Christmas Day they might be alone.'

'Oh, honey,' said her mum with a sigh.

Do some people really have no home to go to?

'Yes, it can be a very lonely city. Come on, the Christmas shopping can wait. Let's go and talk for a moment.'

They walked over to a seat beside a Christmas tree. They could see the whole floor of the toy department. Dolls and teddy bears and hundreds of games and gadgets filled the shelves, and there were people queuing up to buy things.

'So,' said her mum. 'Tell me all about it.'

Ching Ching shrugged. 'I just feel sad. I wish I could do something, but I don't know what.'

'Well, maybe there is something we can do,' said her mum.

'Really?' said Ching Ching, brightening

for a moment. 'Can we go and find the man, and help him? He could live with us.'

'No, I don't think we can quite manage that,' said her mum.

'So what can we do?' asked Ching Ching.

'I'll make you a deal,' said her mum. 'We'll do our Christmas shopping, and then we'll have dinner with the others. Then tomorrow, you and I will spend the morning thinking of a plan. OK?'

Ching Ching thought about it. Her mum was a teacher and was very smart. If anyone could find a way to help others, it was her mum.

The Christmas decorations in the store suddenly looked a bit brighter, and the dolls looked a bit more beautiful than before.

'OK!' she said.

Chapter Six

Once her mum said they would think about the problem in the morning, Ching Ching could enjoy the rest of the night.

She found a cool pink-and-purple tie for her dad, a new football for William, cricket gloves for Henry and some wax for Daniel's surfboard.

They all met back at the main doors.

Ching Ching and her dad raced back

into the shop to buy her mum's present.
She bought a small bottle of perfume in a
box with pretty white flowers on it. Then
they hurried back to the others.

Everyone was hungry!

At the restaurant, Ching Ching had her favourite meal – honey chicken and rice. But even though she was eating and talking and laughing with everyone else, part of her was thinking about how lucky she was, and how not everybody had a family as nice as hers. Some people had no family at all.

It was a horrible thought. She leant over and quickly kissed Henry on the cheek.

'Hey! What was that for?' asked Henry.

'Nothing,' said Ching Ching.

'What was what?' asked Daniel, who was sitting on the other side of Ching Ching. His mouth was full of noodles.

'Not with your mouth full, thanks,' said her dad, just like he always did at home.

'Ching Ching just kissed me!' said Henry.

'Well, so what?' said Ching Ching. 'I don't care. I'll kiss you again if I want to, and I'll kiss you too, Daniel, so watch out.'

'No, thanks,' said Daniel, going back to his noodles.

'You can kiss me anytime,' said William.

'And me,' said her mum.

'Me too!' said her dad.

'Yeah, it wasn't a bad kiss,' admitted Henry.

'Oh, go on then,' said Daniel. 'Come here!'

He pounced on Ching Ching and gave her a big, sticky, noodle-y kiss on her cheek.

'Yuk!' said Ching Ching, laughing.

The train trip home seemed much longer than the trip into town.

Ching Ching's feet ached, and she was ready for bed ages before they finally got to the station.

Then they still had to drive home.

Ching Ching watched the moon through the back window of the car and was almost asleep by the time they pulled into the driveway.

'Don't get up,' said her dad, as he reached in and undid her seatbelt. 'I'll carry you to bed.'

Ching Ching loved being carried to bed. She snuggled against her dad's chest, and soon she was on her bed and her dad was slipping off her shoes.

What a day!

'Did you have a good time?' her dad whispered, as he tucked her into bed.

'Mmm,' smiled Ching Ching, as she fell asleep.

Chapter Seven

Ching Ching woke early the next morning with an uncomfortable feeling. Soon she realised what it was.

Ugh! She had slept in her clothes.

She felt all creased and her hair was full of knots. She sat up in bed, trying to untangle her hair with her fingers. Her backpack was by her desk, bulging with the presents she had bought last night.

She thought about what she had chosen for everyone, and how great Christmas was going to be. Then she remembered something else – today she and her mum were going to work on a plan to help lonely people at Christmas.

She jumped out of bed, suddenly excited. As she ran along the corridor, her mum came out of the bathroom. Her mum was in her dressing gown, and her hair was wrapped in a towel.

'Morning, sweetheart,' said her mum. 'Did you sleep well?'

'Yes,' said Ching Ching, 'but we have to get to work on our project!'

'Well, have breakfast first, honey,' said

her mum. 'And I'll get dressed. We've got loads of time.'

Ching Ching never knew why people always said there was plenty of time. As far as she was concerned, the only time worth bothering about was now!

Still, she might as well have something to eat if her mum was going to be mucking around getting dressed. She finished in the bathroom and then went out to the kitchen.

'Morning, chook,' said her dad, sitting at the table drinking his coffee. 'Still in last night's gear, I see.'

Ching Ching looked down at her crumpled dress.

'Mum tells me that the two of you are

working on a special project this morning,'
her dad went on.

'Yes,' said Ching Ching.

'That's good,' said her dad, gulping
down the last of the coffee and getting up
to wash his mug. 'Christmas is more than
just presents and fairy lights, isn't it?'

Ching Ching wasn't really sure what
he meant, and she was too busy looking
for her favourite cereal bowl to ask.

'Where is everyone?' she asked, when
she had found her bowl and filled it with
cereal and milk.

'The boys got up early and caught the
bus to the beach,' said her dad. 'And I'm
going out in a minute to play golf with

your Uncle Geoff, so you and Mum will have some peace and quiet.'

A whole day with Mum all to herself! That hardly ever happened.

Girls only day!

Now, as long as the phone didn't ring, and the boys didn't need to be picked up, and the car didn't suddenly break down ...

Ching Ching's mum came into the kitchen. Instead of the boring clothes she wore to work, she was wearing bright, comfortable holiday clothes.

'OK, Ching Ching,' she said. 'If you've finished your breakfast, let's get started!'

Chapter Eight

Ching Ching put her bowl in the dishwasher and followed her mum into the study. They cleared the big desk together and sat down.

'Right, let's get down to business.'

Her mum pushed some coloured pens across the desk to Ching Ching and unrolled a sheet of butcher's paper between them.

'This is for writing down our ideas,'

said her mum. 'Anything that helps us think about the problem.'

Ching Ching nodded. She took the lid off the green pen and wrote 'Christmas' on her side of the paper. She drew a wiggly blue line underneath it, and then looked at her mum.

'I can't think of anything else,' she said.

'Well,' said her mum. 'We've done the hardest part. We already know what the problem is. We don't think anyone should be lonely on Christmas Day, right?'

'Right,' said Ching Ching. She wrote 'lonely' in purple pen and drew a sad face next to it.

'But we have to remember that we

can't fix *everything* and we can't help everyone. Agreed?'

Ching Ching nodded. 'As long as we can do *something*, that's better than nothing, isn't it?' she asked.

'Definitely! Anything is better than nothing,' said her mum. 'Now, what do you think makes people feel happy, and loved, on Christmas Day?'

'Presents!' said Ching Ching. 'They make you really happy.'

'Write it down,' said her mum. 'What else?'

'Special yummy food,' said Ching Ching.

'Excellent,' said her mum. 'I'll write that one down.'

'Everyone being together?'

'Yes, yes!' said her mum, writing as fast as she could, as Ching Ching's ideas came more quickly.

'Being glad you have a family,' said Ching Ching.

'That's a really important one,' said her

mum. 'I'm going to underline that idea twice.'

They sat back and looked at their page of thoughts about Christmas.

'Now what?' said Ching Ching.

'Now we figure out how to put our ideas into action,' said her mum. 'How can we help someone who is lonely have some of these good things at Christmas?'

'Well, we can't give everyone a present,' said Ching Ching. 'I've already spent all my money.'

'No,' agreed her mum.

'And we can't give everyone a new family,' said Ching Ching.

'No,' said her mum. 'But remember,

we're not thinking about everyone. We can start smaller.'

'And we can't even tell the people who are on their own that they have to go and be friends with the other lonely people.'

'No,' said her mum. 'But we could invite someone to be with us, couldn't we? Someone could join our family for Christmas Day.'

'Really?' said Ching Ching. 'We can invite someone to our Christmas lunch?'

'Sure,' said her mum.

'Cool,' said Ching Ching. 'But who?'

Chapter Nine

Who can we invite to our Christmas lunch, wondered Ching Ching. It would be different having a stranger at the family meal with them.

Ching Ching was used to having every Christmas exactly the same, with everyone sitting at the same place at the table.

What would it be like to have someone new there?

'You know who might like to come?' said her mum. 'What about Mrs Brand?'

Mrs Brand was an old lady who lived all by herself. She had a rickety old cottage over the back fence from their house.

When Ching Ching was little she used to think Mrs Brand was a bit spooky because she lived with so many cats and always wore black. Her husband had died years ago, before Ching Ching was even born.

Ching Ching had never stopped to think about whether Mrs Brand liked living with only cats for company.

'Yes, let's invite Mrs Brand!' said Ching Ching. 'Do you think she'd want to come?'

'We can only ask,' said her mum. 'Let's walk around after lunch.'

After lunch, Ching Ching and her mum walked around the block to Mrs Brand's house.

It looked even more rickety and spooky up close. There were piles of newspapers tied up in bundles on the front verandah.

Ching Ching's mum knocked on the front door.

Ching Ching looked around to see how many of Mrs Brand's cats she could count. There were three tabbies on the

How many cats
does she have?

front wall, and there was a black-and-white cat in the driveway. A grey cat peered out through the window.

There was no sign of anyone inside the house. Ching Ching was beginning to think Mrs Brand was out.

'I'll just knock again,' said her mum.

'She might have been out in the backyard when we knocked the first time – '

At the very instant she raised her hand to knock again, the door opened a crack and one eye appeared.

'Yes? Hello?' said a croaky voice.

It was Mrs Brand.

Chapter Ten

'Oh, good afternoon, Mrs Brand,' said Ching Ching's mum. 'It's Helen Adams from over the back fence. And I've brought my daughter Ching Ching with me.'

The front door opened a bit more, and Ching Ching saw Mrs Brand standing there in her nightdress. A tortoiseshell cat rubbed itself against her legs.

'Hello, Helen,' said Mrs Brand, smiling.

'Is that really Ching Ching you have with you? Gracious, you've grown, child. You'll have to excuse me, dears, but I've only just got out of bed.'

Ching Ching was a bit embarrassed. She was used to seeing Mrs Brand looking very stern and formal in her stiff black dresses. It didn't seem right to be seeing her in her nightie, with her hair all messy.

'Have you been unwell?' asked her mum, sounding worried.

'No, no,' laughed Mrs Brand. 'I've been reading. I borrowed a book from the library and it's so good I can't put it down. I kept meaning to get out of bed but I wanted to find out what happened next! Oh, but look at me — leaving you standing on the front step. Come in, come in, and I'll make you a cup of tea.'

'That would be lovely,' said Ching Ching's mum, stepping inside.

Ching Ching had never been inside Mrs Brand's house before. She wondered what it would be like.

Inside, Ching Ching got quite a surprise when she looked around. Although the house was a bit spooky from the outside, the inside was totally different.

There were vases of flowers on the tables, lacy cushions on the chairs, and bookcases everywhere. The bookcases were full of books, as well as other things, like

tiny glass animals, candlesticks, thimbles, teacups and matching saucers, interesting shells and pebbles.

At the end of one shelf there was a wedding photo. The lady in the photo was wearing a lovely white dress, and was smiling up at the man beside her. He looked really happy, too, and was smiling back down at the lady.

Ching Ching was dying to go over and

take a closer look, but her mum and Mrs Brand had already walked on into the kitchen so she followed them through.

In the kitchen, a yellow cat sat on the edge of the sink and a shaggy long-haired one lurked under the table. Mrs Brand put on the kettle to boil.

Little pots of violets stood in a row behind the sink, and above the window Mrs Brand had three dinner plates painted with horses.

'So nice to have visitors,' said Mrs Brand. 'I think I've got some shortbread in a tin somewhere ... '

Ching Ching glanced up at her mum. She didn't like tea or shortbread.

Would she have to have some too?

Her mum winked.

'We can't stay too long, Mrs Brand,' she said. 'Ching Ching and I have some chores we have to do this afternoon, but we wanted to see if you had plans for Christmas tomorrow.'

'Plans?' said Mrs Brand. 'Oh, no plans. I usually heat up a tin of plum pudding to have with the cats, but other than that, no plans.'

'Well, Ching Ching and I would love to invite you to have Christmas lunch with us.'

'Oh, I couldn't!' said Mrs Brand. 'It's very kind of you, but I couldn't leave the cats. And I wouldn't want to put you out.'

Ching Ching couldn't think of anything sadder than Mrs Brand alone with her cats on Christmas Day. She wasn't sure what tinned plum pudding tasted like, but it didn't sound very nice.

I don't want Mrs Brand to be alone.

'Please, Mrs Brand,' said Ching Ching. 'Mum and I could pick you up in the car and drop you home again. You'd have such a nice time with us. And we're going to have trifle.'

'Trifle, eh?' Mrs Brand said, with a smile. 'I do like trifle. Well, if you're sure you don't mind? Oh, that would be lovely. Yes, I'd love to come for Christmas lunch.'

'Oh, thank you!' said Ching Ching. 'It's going to be great, I can tell.'

Chapter Eleven

That afternoon was very busy. Ching Ching picked flowers and interesting twigs out of the garden and made a huge posy. Her mum made a batch of shortbread. The flowers and the shortbread would be their Christmas present for Mrs Brand.

Then, while her mum washed up, Ching Ching made Mrs Brand a Christmas card.

She drew a picture of a horse and a cat, together by a Christmas tree.

Mrs Brand will love this!

The sun was going down and it was beginning to get cooler when Ching Ching's brothers got home from the beach.

It was time to wrap the presents and put them under the tree. Everyone went to their own rooms so they could wrap in secret.

Ching Ching had just finished putting a bow on her last present when her dad knocked on her door.

'How are you getting on in there?' asked her dad, peeping around the doorway. 'Nearly done?'

'Nearly,' said Ching Ching.

'Hurry up, then,' he said. 'Your mum needs the wrapping paper, and then we're all going to toast the Christmas tree with eggnog before bed.'

'Eggnog!' said Ching Ching, scrambling to her feet.

William, Henry and Daniel were already in the living room putting their presents under the tree when Ching Ching got there with hers.

Leave some room for my presents!

She tried to guess which ones might be for her, but it was impossible to tell with the boys in the way.

'Can I get past?' she asked. 'I have to put my presents down.'

Henry moved aside and let her kneel down by the tree to find space for her presents. While she was there, she quickly peeked at the cards on the boys' presents, to see which were for her.

'Hey, you! Stop it!' yelled Henry, swooping down on Ching Ching and picking her up. He held her in the air above his head.

'What's up?' asked William.

'Ching Ching is,' laughed Henry.

'Yeah, we can see that,' said Daniel, looking up at Ching Ching.

'She was trying to look at the presents!' said Henry.

'Off-side!' shouted Daniel. 'Not fair!'

'Oh, come on,' said Ching Ching, as she dangled in midair. 'I promise if you let me down, I won't look any more.'

'Promise?' said William. 'You have to cross your heart ... '

'Hey, you kids,' said Mum, struggling towards the tree with her arms full of presents. 'What's going on?'

'Nothing,' said William.

'Just giving Ching Ching a special Christmas hug,' said Henry, letting Ching Ching down, but only so he could wrap her tightly in his arms instead.

'Mm-mmf!' said Ching Ching, muffled by Henry's hug.

'Henry, I don't think your sister can

quite breathe in there,' said Mum. 'Anyway, Daniel, go to the kitchen and get the glasses. It's time for eggnog, and then bed.'

After they all had eggnog, and toasted the Christmas tree, Ching Ching brushed her teeth and got into her pyjamas. She climbed into bed and switched off the light, but there's nothing harder than trying to fall asleep on Christmas Eve.

Ching Ching tossed and turned. She got up and had a drink of water, and went to the toilet about four times. Eventually she gave up on sleeping and read in bed.

'Are you still up?' whispered her mum, stopping by on her way to bed.

'I can't sleep,' Ching Ching whispered back, giggling.

'I know,' said her mum. 'It's hard, isn't it? But see if you can drop off now.'

Chapter Twelve

Ching Ching woke the next morning to the sound of Henry and William wrestling in the hall. Daniel was cheering them on.

'Grab his foot! No, the other foot!'

Ching Ching leapt out of bed and ran out. Daniel was now on the floor, too, wrestling in a mad three-way tangle of bodies and laughter.

'Merry Christmas!' yelled Ching Ching,

throwing herself on top of the pile and trying to kiss and tickle her brothers at the same time.

Merry Christmas!

'What's all this?' asked Dad, coming out into the hall.

'Oh, ouch!' yelped William. 'It's Ching Ching, Dad! She's beating us all up.'

'Yes, make her stop!' said Henry. 'She's too rough.'

'And on Christmas Day, too!' said Daniel.

'All right, Ching Ching,' laughed her dad. 'The boys have had enough for now. Let them up, will you? There's a pet.'

Ching Ching got up off the floor, and her brothers picked themselves up, too.

'Phew! Thanks,' said William.

'Where's Mum?' asked Henry.

'In the kitchen, I bet,' said Daniel.

'Yes,' said Dad. 'She's been up for hours, getting things ready for lunch.'

'Lunch?' said Daniel. 'Who cares about lunch? We want presents!'

'That's the spirit,' said Dad dryly. 'Come on, then. Let's get your mum away from the kitchen and go and sit by the tree.'

William and Henry raced to the kitchen and between them picked up Mum and carried her to the Christmas tree.

'But I've still got my apron on!' Mum protested. 'And my hands are wet from peeling potatoes!'

The Christmas tree looked wonderful. The fairy lights were flashing, the tinsel was sparkling, and underneath were all the presents, beautifully wrapped and waiting to be opened.

'All right, then,' said Mum. 'Merry Christmas! Let's open those presents!'

For a while it was chaos. Six people swapping presents and kisses, a flurry of unwrapping, and everyone shouting, 'Thanks!'

Wrapping paper and ribbon flew everywhere. Ching Ching's dad said he loved his tie, and William and Henry started playing with William's new football straight away, nearly knocking the gingerbread house off its table.

'Ching Ching, this perfume's lovely,' said her mum, but Ching Ching hardly noticed. She was too excited about her present from her mum and dad. A pink helmet and – she could hardly believe it – a skateboard!

It had been a fantastic Christmas already, thought Ching Ching. And the day had only just begun.

Chapter Thirteen

'You'd better go and change out of your pyjamas, Ching Ching,' said her mum. 'It's about time to go and fetch Mrs Brand.'

Ching Ching got dressed in about thirty seconds flat. She put her helmet on too.

'That was fast,' said her mum. 'And I see you've brought your skateboard.'

'I thought I'd skate around to Mrs Brand's house,' said Ching Ching. 'It's only one block, so I don't even have to cross the road.'

'All right,' said her mum. 'And then you can ride in the car on the way home.'

It was a short drive to Mrs Brand's house, but a long journey by skateboard. Ching Ching fell off six times, but she didn't care. She loved the feeling as she rolled along the footpath.

When she got to Mrs Brand's house, her mum was already there, waiting by the front gate with Mrs Brand. She was dressed all in black as usual, but as she came closer, Ching Ching saw she was wearing some dangly earrings shaped like Christmas trees.

'Merry Christmas, Mrs Brand,' said
Ching Ching. 'Did you see what I got
from Mum and Dad?'

'Yes,' said Mrs Brand. 'You looked very fast and daring coming around the corner.'

'Did you fall?' asked her mum.

'Hardly at all,' said Ching Ching.

They got into the car. Mrs Brand sat in the front with Mum, and Ching Ching sat behind.

'Now, Ching Ching,' said Mrs Brand, turning to see Ching Ching sitting in the back seat. 'I don't know anything about boys these days, so I'm afraid I haven't brought your brothers anything, but I do have a little something for you.'

She passed Ching Ching a flat, square present. It was wrapped in old, creased paper with kittens on it.

'Oh, Mrs Brand, you needn't have done that,' said Ching Ching's mum, but Ching Ching had already thanked her and taken the present, unwrapping it eagerly.

It was an old book, a bit battered on the corners, but with the most beautiful picture of a black horse on the cover.

'*Black Beauty*!' breathed Ching Ching in delight. 'My friend Iris says this is the best book ever. Even better than *The Black Stallion*!'

'Ah, good,' said Mrs Brand. 'I thought you might like that one. I was given that when I was your age. Look in the front.'

Ching Ching opened the cover and saw some old-fashioned, faded writing.

To darling Edna,
　　　on Christmas Day,

Something for you to read in the two or three minutes each day you aren't out with Tully or getting yourself into mischief!

　　　With all my love,
　　　Auntie Rebecca

'Oh, thank you,' said Ching Ching, trying to imagine old Mrs Brand as a girl her age. 'I can't wait to read it.'

Chapter Fourteen

Christmas lunch was loud, happy and delicious. They all pulled crackers, and even Mrs Brand wore her silly paper crown. Ching Ching sat next to her and while they were eating, Mrs Brand told her all sorts of stories.

After lunch, the boys went swimming and Ching Ching practised with her skateboard up and down the driveway.

She was starting to get pretty good!

'Ching Ching,' her mum called out. 'It's time to take Mrs Brand home. She needs to feed her cats.'

They drove slowly back to Mrs Brand's house.

'Thank you, Helen,' said Mrs Brand. 'I've had a lovely day. And thank you, Ching Ching. I love my flowers and I'm going to put my Christmas card right by my bed so I can see it when I wake up.'

'I'll draw you an even better one when you come for Christmas next year,' said Ching Ching.

They waved goodbye, waiting until Mrs Brand was safely inside.

'Well,' said her mum, as they drove back, 'another Christmas over.'

'But Christmas isn't really over,' said Ching Ching. 'We've still got dinner tonight, and then Boxing Day tomorrow, and all the leftovers to eat – '

'Urgh! Stop,' groaned her mum. 'Please don't talk about food again at least until January.'

'Why?' asked Ching Ching. 'I'm starving. I hope the others haven't finished the trifle while we've been gone. And then there's the gingerbread house – '

'Ching Ching!' said her mum. 'I mean it. You eat if you have to, but don't tell me about it, please.'

Ching Ching was quiet for a moment, dreaming of gingerbread.

'Now, tell me,' said her mum. 'Did you have a good day?'

'Oh, yes!' said Ching Ching. 'I love my skateboard, and Mrs Brand was really funny. Did you know when she was my age, she had a horse called Tully and they were going to run away together so she didn't have to go to school anymore?'

'No, I didn't,' said her mum.

'Yeah,' Ching Ching went on, 'and then when she was Daniel's age, she got bitten by a snake and had to stay in hospital for seven weeks, and after that she thought going to school wasn't so bad after all.'

'Really?' said her mum. 'It sounds like you two had a good chat.'

'Yes,' said Ching Ching. 'I'm really glad she came.'

They arrived back home. Ching Ching's dad was playing football in the front garden with William, Henry and Daniel. Ching Ching leapt out of the car to join in.

'Yeah!' she yelled as she was tackled by Daniel and sat on by Henry. 'Ouch! This was the best Christmas ever!'

Merry Christmas, Go Girls!

Collect them all!

go girl

Sleep-over

Boy friend?

Surf's Up

Sister Spirit

Dancing Queen

Flower Girl

Camp Chaos

Back to School

The Worst Gymnast

Sink or Swim

Birthday Girl

Music Mad

www.gogirlhq.com

Tweenie Genie

Poppy is just an ordinary girl. The only thing strange about her is that she's great at squeezing into small spac—

So it's a pretty big shock when she finds out she's a genie! Suddenly she has to get used to wearing high ponytails, riding magic carpets and granting wishes.

At least squeezing into into a tiny genie bottle comes naturally!

FAIRY SCHOOL Drop-out

Elly hates being a fairy – all those
itchy tutus and boring spells.
It's not nearly as fun as skateboarding.
Follow Elly the Fairy school drop-out
on all her fabulous adventures.